The Dollhouse

Sabine Ritchie

Contents

Chapter 1

Taito pictured above.

It was the feeling of rain constantly hitting his face in a steady stream that alerted his consciousness that he had spent the night outside. The young man still refused to completely awaken at this point, simply turning his head to the side to avoid the brunt of the rain continuing to trickle into his eyes. However, the heavens were not content with this, as only moments later his beta's voice was ringing in his head, demanding to know where he was. The young man sighed, sitting up fully and dragging a hand down his face. He knew the only reason he was still alone was because the rain made it difficult to track his scent this far into the forest surrounding their territory. He thanked whoever was listening for that small mercy, before begrudgingly answering Matt, his beta, and letting him know he would be back soon. The young man stretched, relishing the satisfying pop of his spine aligning. Wasting no more time, he turned to his right and began the trek home, deciding against sluggish movements as his discomfort was not at the forefront of his mind. His clothes stuck deliciously to his person, revealing the natural physique every male wolf was blessed with once they came of age. His muscles bulged with the simple action of walking, his eight pack now on full display for any wandering eyes. His was a warrior pack, so years of training had perfected and sculpted what nature had already blessed him with. His closed cropped midnight black hair was heavy with rain, his strong jaw clenched in irritation. He transferred to a light jog, the idea of a nice hot shower more appealing the longer he moved through the rain-drenched forest.

It was considerably darker when he burst from the forest, his beta and third in command swarming him immediately. He shrugged them off, not listening as they tried to catch him up to speed on what he'd missed during his impromptu day off. Once he got inside the pack house, Mary, the beta's mate, wordlessly offered him a towel, a knowing glint in her eye as she went back into the kitchen to talk to the cook, Tabitha. The young man smirked, gratefully drying himself as best as he could, making a beeline for his room. Of course, Matt and Ramon, his third in command, followed along after him, not caring that he began to strip as they continued to ramble.

"Taito, you need to stop pretending to ignore us. The rouge problem has been handled for now and they're relatively peaceful. Now you still have paperwork to do, as well as some other things you need to take care of." Ramon stated blandly, completely ignoring the resolute slam of the bathroom door. Matt sighed tiredly, flopping onto the king-sized bed in the middle of the room.

"One day he won't be able to avoid us. Who elected him again?" Ramon rolled his eyes but shot a smirk Matt's way.

"He'll get it done when he gets out of the shower. He can only put it off for so long." Matt pouted but sighed, silently agreeing with Ramon.

"Let's go eat. The idiot will do his work with or without us and I'm starving!" Both men stood to their feet and headed back downstairs, appearing in the kitchen to look for leftovers from lunch.

Chapter 2

R amon pictured above.

Ana sighed as she walked out of the convenience store, another failed job interview. She hadn't meant to yell at the man, but they had been subtly insulting her throughout the interview. She had never been able to keep her mouth shut, but she had tried until the last slimy comment had slithered from his slightly chapped lips. That had been more than she could take, so she had reacted before her mind could conjure a biting but polite comment in reply.

It was because of this she found herself walking home in the night, the streets much quieter than they should have been. Ana didn't notice at first, but then the hairs on the back of her neck began to raise. Her arms began to tingle, her nerves alight with the adrenaline beginning to pump through her veins. Ana shivered, her eyes darting back and forth. The street was suddenly too abandoned. There were no stores on this side of town, only a few modest residential houses. She could feel the tension in her shoulders, hear the Jaw's theme song begin in her head. Ana quickened her pace, thanking the gods above she decided to wear exercise clothes to the store.

She changed to a light jog down the street, eyeing the windows of her neighbors, mentally noting which houses still had lights on. She was five blocks away when her mental soundtrack picked up the tempo. Her house was in sight just before the climax. Heart pounding, as her pace had changed with the music, her hand was just reaching for the door handle when the climax hit. Ana burst through the door with the grace of a newborn lamb, but her sigh of relief was loud and thankful.

She put away her groceries and moved into the living room, where an envelope sat suspiciously in the middle of her coffee table. It was because of this envelope she didn't see the man creeping stealthily behind her. He didn't even give her time to scream before a practiced hand moved the cloth over her mouth, effectively knocking her out. Ana's body went limp, and the intruder gathered her gently into his arms before swiping the keys off her counter. He locked the door behind them, put Ana in the passenger seat, and started the car, driving off to their destination.

Chapter 3

Ana awoke with her head pounding and dizziness clouding her eyes. The room she found herself in was more of a cell than a room. The dirt beneath her feet slipped between her toes. The bars seemed to be slightly rusted, but not enough to aid in any escape attempts. She twisted her head behind her as far as it would go and saw concrete walls. Looking up gave her a view of another concrete structure, so it seemed safe to assume she was underground. Now that she had regained consciousness, she became aware of the strain her arms. They were chained above her head, handcuffed together with the handcuffs linked to a chain hanging from the ceiling. Her feet were free, but that neither helped nor hindered her current situation. From what she could tell she had been placed in the middle of the cell, so she couldn't use anything to lean against or stand on to help soothe her screaming muscles. Ana sighed and experimentally pulled on her arms. She almost fell over in surprise when her arms came down to rest in front of her, the chain extending to accommodate this new position. I wonder... Ana took a few experimental steps, the chain again extending to compensate. She found she could walk all the way to the wall, but the chain stopped right before she got close enough to the bars to touch them.

She sighed and walked back towards the wall, leaning against it and letting her arms dangle listlessly in front of her body. Footsteps soon alerted her to the fact she wasn't as alone as she had initially believed. Steeling herself by taking a few deep breaths, she looked towards the bars, the elongating shadow dancing across the floor her only indication that someone was slowly approaching. Just as she felt the anticipation would kill her, her downcast gaze caught steel toed combat boots stop in front of her cell.

"Ah you're awake. Good deal. This will make this go by much faster." Ana looked up as the deep voice reverberated around the room. She was met with the sight of a man standing proudly at six feet, with jet black hair jelled back and to the side. His clothes were impeccable on his toned body, relaxed muscles flexing as he clasped his hands behind his back. He was wearing a pressed white collared shirt over distressed jeans, which laid over his black combat boots. He was handsome, but she went for the tall, dark, and brooding with a tragic past. This man just had a slightly crazed gleam in his eye, so she definitely wasn't interested. She had been so busy checking out the man who spoken, she didn't even notice the second man standing imposingly, half covered in shadow. Ana didn't have time to notice anything other than his striking green eyes before the first man unlocked the cell door, walking in and grasping her chin delicately, turning it this way and that.

"Hey! What gives?!" The man only chuckled, before moving on to her arms, poking and prodding like she was some kind of animal on display. He grinned once he was done, seemingly satisfied.

"Yes, you'll do nicely my dear. Tony, go and get my things from the back room, would you? I would like to start immediately." The man hidden in shadow nodded once before slipping away, returning shortly with a rolling tray and multiple medical tools. Ana eyed them warily as Tony put on gloves. "You, my dear, can call me Calvin. We'll be getting to know each other very well." He smirked devilishly before pressing a button on the tray, pulling the chain back in so her arms once again were above her head. Ana stubbornly looked to the side, refusing to say a word. Calvin grinned wider, the crazed look in his eyes turning wild. "Oh yes, I'll be having fun with this one. Tony, let's begin."

Chapter 4

Ana was exhausted, mentally and physically. She had already lost track of how long she'd been here. It felt like years, but she knew it was probably closer to a month. Calvin had been relentless, treating her like a science experiment. He was nothing but clinical; once the tests began he had Tony meticulously documenting everything. Sometimes he would test her with the same dose of strange liquid multiple times to be sure of the results. She had long since given up on resisting and escaping, choosing instead to retreat into her mind, or unconsciousness, when the pain became too much. Her throat was raw and hoarse from the screams that ripped from her throat. Tony would take over whenever she teetered on the brink of exhaustion, while Calvin was the lead while she was awake. Both men looked at her with no trace of lust in their eyes, for which she was grateful. Ana knew she would never recover if one of them tried to do that.

It was late one evening when Ana noticed a change was happening to her body. Her wounds were healing right before her eyes, and her appetite grew. The room became clearer day by day, as if her eyes were sharpening. She told Calvin this, while Tony recorded it, both paying her their undivided attention. Ana had learned quickly to cooperate with the two men. Their inhuman strength had frightened her beyond belief. She knew right then that either of them could kill her with the flick of her wrists. Ana sighed and stared at the ceiling while the men shared looks. She had also learned they could converse silently, chalking it up to having worked together for so long. Her head swiveled to look at them when Calvin cleared his throat.

"We've decided that field tests are in order. Be good and don't run now." They freed her from her restraints and Tony helped her off the table. Ana stretched her limbs experimentally, feeling her muscles groan at the first real movement she'd had since she'd been taken. She looked at them confused, walking warily behind them as the group began the trek through the underground prison and to the outside. Ana stopped abruptly and shielded her eyes, letting them adjust before she looked around. The sight that greeted her was a small clearing, a forest beginning at its edge. The only building was the one they had just left, with two doors on its side. She assumed one led to her prison while the other lead to the main part of the house. This explained why it seemed Tony and Calvin never left. Ana looked to Calvin again, awaiting orders. "You are to run as far as you can. If Tony can't find you by sundown, you're free. If he does, we start the next round of tests. Good luck my dear." Ana didn't need to be told twice. She ran like her life depended on it, making a beeline for the trees. Tony let out a howl, letting her know the chase had begun. Ana ran faster, looking desperately for a river or something that would mask her scent. Calvin had explained everything once the tests began. They were werewolves, and the strange liquid they injected her with was a substance called wolfsbane. They wanted to see what it would do to humans, hence why they kidnapped her. Ana had been randomly selected based on medical data, such as her health, mental state, and gender. She realized it must be the wolfsbane that was enhancing her senses and causing the other changes in her body. There was no other explanation. She would never turn into a wolf, however. Calvin explained that since she hadn't been born one, there was no way to turn her. The effects seemed more closely to mirror Captain America's transformation. Her senses were enhanced, but she didn't immediately gain muscle mass, although her body toned itself up. Ana spotted a tree that was hidden partially behind two others. She changed course and was just beginning to shimmy up the tree when a hand grasped her ankle, yanking her back down. Tony stared stonily down at her, throwing her over his shoulder. Ana screamed and cried, the adrenaline fading as her defeat settled in her bones. Neither noticed the glowing pair of eyes that silently melted back into the foliage.

Chapter 5

Ana's days blended together into months, then years as the experiments continued. She could hide for longer periods, but Tony always found her in the end. She knew it was ultimately because of her scent. There was nothing to mask it with, so running through different parts of the forest before selecting a hiding spot only delayed the inevitable. Every time she was caught they brought her back down to her cell, allowing her a small break to eat, rehydrate, and catch her breath.

It was one such night, Ana lying awake as she leaned against the wall. She didn't know what had woken her, but now she was alert. Tony and Calvin had finished earlier, leaving her to her own devices for the rest of the night. She hummed to herself, even as the hairs on the back of her neck began to rise. Her body was aware of something her mind hadn't realized yet, and when Ana realized she had curled further into the shadows and ceased humming, her body poised to strike, she became more alert and on edge than ever before. She waited in the darkness with baited breath, eyes darting from her trapped hands to the cell door. An explosion soon rocked the house, followed by shouting and snarling. Ana didn't know whether she should call out or remain silent, deciding on the latter since the new people could be just as dangerous if not more so than Calvin and

Tony. Snarls and growls continued to rip through the building before she heard two screams of agony. Ana shut her eyes and curled further in on herself until both abruptly cut off. Voices now echoed through the house, and she heard footsteps approaching her cell. Ana inhaled sharply before straightening, not wanting these strangers to see her fear. She held her breath and squinted as a flashlight suddenly shone in her face.

"Alpha, we have a girl down here!" Ana blinked and looked away from the light. Suddenly a strong, commanding voice rang out.

"MINE!" Ana stoppedbreathing.

Chapter 6

She was silent as they freed her and brought her above ground. The one who had claimed her, who she learned was the alpha, stuck to her like glue. Ana stayed perfectly calm, casually glancing around. She was looking for the perfect moment to escape. It was obvious from the previous scuffle inside the house that these men were also werewolves. Her nightmare wouldn't end if she allowed herself to be captured again. Her moment came when the alpha turned around to talk to someone. Ana bolted, ignoring the shouts and angry snarls demanding she come back. She silently thanked Calvin and Tony for all those games of hide and seek. She tore through the forest, seeing the first rays of daylight through breaks in the trees. Heart pounding, Ana pushed herself to go as fast as she could. She could hear her pursuers gaining ground. Ana assumed they must have shifted, otherwise she would've had more distance between them. A road slowly came into view. With newfound hope, she put on a burst of speed and sprinted towards it. She could practically taste her freedom as her bare feet ate up the distance. Almost there... She was just about to make it when a body slammed into her side, violently knocking the wind out of her. They landed harshly on the forest floor. When Ana looked at the man on top of her and saw it was the alpha, she screamed. All the fight left her as she screamed her frustration and bitterness, tears pouring from her eyes. The alpha just picked her up, wrapping her in his coat and his arms before running to the side, parallel to the road but deeper into the forest. Eventually, Ana just fell silent, exhausted but refusing sleep. With Calvin and Tony, she knew they weren't interested in trying anything. What they did was wrong, but she was comforted in the knowledge she always knew what to expect. These men were uncharted territory. The alpha kept glancing at her but she stubbornly refused to meet his gaze. She had no idea why he'd claimed her, but she knew it probably meant either more experiments or confinement.

Her hard, empty gaze took in the pack house and all the wolves spilling from it. She was silent as people looked at her curiously. Silent as the alpha claimed her to be his mate and their luna. Silent as the people cheered and congratulated their alpha. Silent as he moved fluidly up the stairs and into what she could only assume was his room. Silent as he placed her gently on the bed. He sat next to her and reached over to cup her face. Ana turned away and scooted over, not wanting his touch. She heard a sigh but refused to look at him until he gently toughed her shoulder.

"Why won't you speak? Why were you down there? Do you – "

"Can I go home now?" His face looked stricken for a moment before he grabbed her hands, smiling apologetically.

"I'm sorry, but I can'tallow that. You belong here with me - "Ana snatched her hands away and stood,heading for the bathroom. She ignored him as he called out to her. She closedand locked the door before breaking into sobs. I just want to go home! I never asked for any of this

Chapter 7

She stayed in that bathroom for hours. The only reason she finally emerged was because her hunger had finally gotten the best of her. When she opened the door, she wasn't surprised to see the alpha wasn't in the room. She kept her guard up as she poked her head out the door to the hallway, glancing around before walking out. She walked down the stairs and turned right, finding another long hallway. It's almost like one of those scenes from a horror movie. The only difference is the lighting. Once at the end of the hall she took another right, stumbling upon the dining room and kitchen. There was a bar counter that acted as a separator for the kitchen and dining hall. The dining hall was large and open. Long, mahogany tables sat in the center. There were three rows of about six tables. Benches with a glossy finish served as chairs. The walls were a calming shade of light brown. There were skylights installed in the ceiling to allow natural light to seep in as it pleased. The kitchen was modern – sleek countertops and updated appliances. The countertops were granite, complementing the stainless-steel appliances. The floor was mahogany wood with a marble finish – matching the dining room décor. There was an island in the middle with a few backless bar stools accompanying it. Ana opened the fridge and the pantry, getting out ingredients for pancakes. She bustled around the kitchen, humming to herself as she worked. She had just finished her first batch, the delicious smell wafting over and around her, when she heard shuffling coming from behind the bar counter. Ana whirled around, but no one was there. She was turning back around when she saw a foot sticking out. She held in a laugh and put down the spatula before padding over. She may be cautious and guarded while she was held captive here, but she always had a soft spot for kids.

"Would you like some? I made too much batter for just myself anyway. The kids jumped, startled, before shyly nodding their heads. Ana grinned and stood up, heading back into the kitchen with the children following behind her. They scrambled onto the bar stools and watched her eagerly. Ana went back to cooking and humming.

"What song is that? It's pretty." Ana put the finished stacks of pancakes on plates and handed them to the children along with syrup. She then grabbed her own food and perched on the last available bar stool.

"I'm not sure. My mother always used to hum it whenever she cooked."

"Oh. My mom does that sometimes. She's really pretty. Is your mom pretty?" Ana smiled wistfully.

"The most beautiful woman in the world." They finished eating in silence after that. The children thanked her for the food and helped clear the table before scampering off. She washed the dishes and sighed to herself. Now what? She didn't want to risk running into that alpha, or anyone else honestly, but she also didn't want to stay cooped up in that room. She paced the length of the kitchen, trying to make up her mind. Well I could always- She thoughts were cut off by a massive yawn. Well I guess that settles that. She headed out of the kitchen and up the stairs, pausing at the top. Did I take a left or a right in that last hallway? Ana was severely directionally challenged, which explained why she was still with the wolves. When she'd been taken the first time, she'd woken up seemingly halfway through and managed to catch glimpses out the window of some of the surrounding area before they'd entered the woods. So, she had known if she could find the road, help wasn't far. But here, she had no clue what was around. Although she had been awake the entire journey, the men she'd traveled with had put her in the middle of the back seat, and used their stature to block the windows. She could see through parts of the windshield, but they hadn't passed any street signs. Before they'd entered the cars, the alpha had taken her deeper into the forest and out the other side to a long dirt road where the cars were waiting.

While she had beenzoning out, she'd taken a wrong turn somewhere and ended up in theentertainment room. There was a bright red popcorn machine in the corner, withplush recliners set at different heights like in the movie theaters in front ofthat. At the very front of the room, past the three small steps on the lowestrow of seats, a large, wall mounted projector screen took up almost the fulllength of the wall, with a few feet of wall space on either side. Ana staredwide eyed around the room. How in Hadesdid I even get here?! Stupidridiculously large pack house! I just wanna sleep dang it! Those chairs don't lookhalf bad though... Ana shrugged and grabbed the blanket folded neatly in thecorner before making herself comfortable in the last row of chairs. Her eyesclosed almost instantly and she grinned. Nope,not bad at all.

Chapter 8

She woke up to warm hands playing in her hair. She didn't want to wake up - she was warm and more comfortable than she thought she'd be sleeping in a chair. Said chair moved slightly, causing her head to rise before returning to its previous position. Chairs don't move like that. Huh. Wait, chairs don't move like that! Ana shot up so fast she tumbled to the floor. A low chuckle alerted her to her apparent audience. There sat the alpha, still smirking as he offered her a hand. She huffed and stood, ignoring it.

"What do you want?" He grasped his chest dramatically, feigning hurt.

"You wound me! You were the one looking adorable curled up in this chair. How could I possibly resist? Especially when you avoid me while awake." He wiggled his eyebrows while Ana crossed her arms and turned her head stubbornly to the side.

"Of course! You kidnapped me after all." His face fell, but the look was gone in a flash.

"I admit I brought you here due to my selfishness, but you are my mate. I need you. I finally found you after all these years of searching for you. I can't let you go. Not now, not ever!" His eyes blazed during his declaration. So much so that she had to look away. She ignored the tingles shooting up her arms from where his hands grasped hers. He had been so passionate she couldn't bring herself to pull away just yet. That compassion did nothing to dampen the righteous fire blazing in her own gaze.

"You didn't even stop to ask! You just took me. I had just been freed from that place, only to have my freedom stolen again in the blink of any eye! I know what you are, what this place must be. You could have asked me what I wanted after you tackled me. But you didn't. You took me back here, expecting me to love you?! I'm not a werewolf! I can't love a man I don't know." She gently removed his hold on her, exiting the room. Just before she was out of ear shot, the alpha called out to her.

"Taito! That's my name." Ana was angry, but she couldn't help the small smile playing on her lips, even as she ruefully shook her head. She made sure she was alone before testing out his name.

"Taito, huh?"

Chapter 9

Ana wished he'd never told him why she was being cold towards him, and everyone else by association. Ever since that day, pack members came up and introduced themselves before whisking her away for some bonding time. She wouldn't have minded so much if everyone hadn't managed to somehow bring up Taito every chance they got. Sherry, her new self-proclaimed best friend, was the guiltiest of this. The two girls had warmed up to each other surprisingly quickly. After the onslaught of pack members ended, the two began hanging out almost full time. They talked about everything, well Sherry did anyway. Ana had been there almost three months, so she'd lost her hostility towards the pack, but she was still closed off when it came to personal details. She still didn't fully trust them after all – not when nightmares of her time with Calvin and Tony plagued her still. But Ana's wariness of Sherry had nothing to do with her previous captors. Every time they hung out, Sherry would question her on her feelings for the alpha. They would also "mysterious" run into Taito almost every day. Ana was beginning to suspect the mind link she'd read about in books was actually true. She also suspected Taito was shirking his responsibilities. She had wandered into his office on afternoon (she'd found it by accident and given in to her curiosity to go inside). He'd been passed out at his desk, papers, books, and smaller more detailed sections of the maps hung on the wall scattered around him. Ana couldn't help thinking he looked cute, quietly leaving. She may not trust him, but the bond wouldn't let her completely refuse him either.

Late one afternoon, Anadecided she'd go for a short walk. The house had become stifling. She toldSherry before heading out, politely greeting some of the pack on her way. Taitohad been nowhere in sight today, which meant she'd had a break from Sherry'smeddling. She entered the woods, automatically tensing up. Ana knew there werepatrols in the forest with her, but that gave her little piece of mind. She wanderedaround, having no destination in mind. The sun was setting, painting a backdropof red, orange, and dark blue and purple hues against the trees. Ana sighed and-turned around, intending to head back. I'llhave to go out earlier tomorrow. And maybe I can convince Sherry to take meshopping; I can only borrow so many of her clothes. The snapping of a twigbrought her out of her musings. Ana didn't even pause to scan the surroundingsbefore taking off, feet pounding against the underbrush.

Chapter 10

Harsh breaths rushed out of her lungs in rapid succession. The echo of footsteps that were clearly not hers taunted her with their increasing closeness. Maybe it's a patrolman? But then wouldn't he call out? So it's an enemy?! But shouldn't they have been apprehended or something by now? Where's the patrolmen?! Or Taito! That lazy son of a – Ana was violently tackled to the ground, cutting off her mental tirade. Ya know, I'm getting real tired of being attacked like this. She took a deep breath and screamed at the top of her lungs. She bucked like a bull, noticing the grip on her was loosening. Ana violently thrashed until she managed to get an arm free. She jabbed her elbow back hard, landing a blow in the man's gut. She threw her head back, satisfied when the man let out a curse. She rolled away as soon as she was freed, taking off in what was hopefully the direction of the house. The pounding of heavy footsteps starting up again made her rethink her plan. She shimmied up a tree instead, climbing high enough to hide in the leaves. Ana held her breath as the man suddenly burst into view. Panting, he stopped about a few feet from the base of the tree. He slowly scanned the area, grinning when he couldn't find her.

"Good job, Luna! Looks like Taito won't have much to worry about after all." Ana blinked, her brain struggling to make sense of what she'd just heard, adrenaline still rushing through her veins. Good job Luna? Good job Luna...Good job Luna?! Ana's face twisted in rage, her hands shaking. Slowly, she climbed down the tree, stopping when she was standing face to face with her "attacker." He stuck his hand out, a goofy grin plastered on his face – she wanted to smack it into next week. "I'm Thomas, we met when he had that outdoor movie night." Thomas laughed at her blank face. "It was one of the bonding sessions? You, me, Kenya, Denise, Greg, Terry, and Sherry?" Oh, she remembered alright; the expression painted on her face was because Taito was running up, along with Matt and Ramon. She waited until he went to hug her before punching him in the face. Everyone gasped while Ana screamed. It felt like her hand shattered as soon as she'd punched him. Taito rubbed a hand down his face before having the decency to look sheepish.

"I just wanted to show you that you always had to be on guard. You are my Luna now. My enemies will be after you." She glared and cradled her hand.

"Who said I agreed to this meathead?! Idiot! I was seriously scared for my life! Are you trying to give me PTSD?? Have you forgotten where you kidnapped me from?! And where the hell was the patrol? Where the hell were you?! You dare call me your Luna and say I can't leave because you need me, but where were you when I needed you? Hypocritical jerk! Why I – " Taito yanked her to him, minding her hand. He buried his face in her hair and held her.

"I'm sorry love. I was always here, from the moment you screamed. But I needed to see what you would do if I couldn't immediately come to save you. I won't always be close – sometimes you'll have to stall until I get there. But I was watching the whole time. We all were. If something had happened, Thomas would've gotten you to safety. You were never in any real danger. You need to remember this is a warrior pack. Some didn't believe you had the inner strength to lead them, despite that fact you survived what you did. It was cruel, but it was necessary." Ana wanted to be angry, but she understood what he meant. Some people in the pack would look at her like she was weak. They'd whisper to each other when they thought she couldn't hear them. If she was a normal human, she wouldn't. She wasn't though, so she did. The bond also didn't let her keep her anger, especially with Taito being so close.

"You're still a jerk. I'm not apologizing for hitting you." He chuckled at that and ruffled her hair before stepping back.

"Fair enough, but I'm still punishing you for it." That devilish smirk on his lips forced her to look away. She refused to let him see how much that look affected her. The spectators watched in amusement.

"That girl is definitely our Luna. She jabbed me so hard I had to catch my breath a couple of times before running after her. Fast too. Faster than she should be. What'd they do to her?" The others simply shook their heads, smiling when the couple turned to face them. Taito turned to Ana, accidentally grabbing her injured hand. Ana winced, but was otherwise fine. She waved off their concern.

"I heal faster than even you guys do thanks to them so I'll be good as new by the end of the day at the latest." Ana breezed past them before stopping and turning back to face them. "Well don't just stand there. It's not like I know the way back."

Chapter 11

- -

"So, does that mean you can regenerate and stuff too?"

"Don't be silly – I'm not a starfish." Ana had explained to the group her recovery abilities. She had also explained that the wolfsbane Calvin had used had been absorbed fully into her system, which caused her heightened sense and increased recovery rate. A shadow had passed over everyone's face when she told them she basically had wolfsbane coursing through her veins. They'd cast a worried glance at Taito, piquing Ana's curiosity. "Why is everyone looking at you like that?" Taito sighed and ran a hand down his face before answering.

"You know how we're mates? Well to complete the bond I need to bite you. But wolfsbane is poisonous to wolves, so your blood is poison to me. And if I can't complete the process I'll go insane. I won't be able to hold out forever, so either way the bond will be completed."

"So, if we fully mate my blood will kill you?!" Ana was torn – on one hand she was excited that she would have more stall time until they mated. But the other part of her that had been growing day by day wailed in agony at the revelation. All of her though agreed this overall wasn't good news. She didn't want to be a murderer! "So, what can we do? It's a part of me now!" Taito shook his head and grabbed her face softly, leaning forward until their foreheads touched.

"I'm not sure. Don't worry love, we'll figure it out." The others trickled out of the room, giving the couple some privacy. Taito pulled back and looked her over one last time before picking her up bridle style and walking out. Ana sputtered but otherwise didn't complain. The infirmary hadn't been bad until the doctor began questioning her to find out why she was healing faster than even a werewolf. Taito passed by the kitchen, ducking in and dropping her onto a bar stool. Ana squeaked before righting herself. Taito snickered while he bustled around the kitchen. "I'm feeling French toast. Are you okay with that?"

"I'm not all that hungry right now, so you don't have to fix me any. Thank you though."

"You need to eat sweet cheeks. Especially with all that exercise you got in the woods." Ana stuck out her tongue childishly before turning her head, missing the golden flash in Taito's eyes at the action.

"I'm fine. I don't have much of an appetite. And don't call me sweet cheeks!" Taito walked over and stopped in front of her, bracing his hands on either side of her on the counter. His eyes flickered to her lips before settling on her eyes, drowning in them. He put his mouth right next to her ear.

"I know how we can work one up." He pulled back and wiggled his eyebrows. He looked and sounded so tempting in that moment Ana nearly combusted. So, she fell back on her default response – refusal.

"Pervert!" Taito doubled over, laughing so hard tears gathered in the corners of his eyes.

"I c-couldn't help it!" He managed between fits of laughter. "You're so easy to tease. But you seriously need to eat. I won't take no for an answer Ana."

She would never admit it, but she practically fainted when he said her name. She made no more complaints or objections, quietly eating when he handed her a plate. She wasn't sure if she could handle another attack like that. Stupid man with his stupid sexy voice...and body...and those eyes – OKAY THAT'S ENOUGH! Once done eating, she took her plate to the sink and washed it. Ana turned toward him and sighed.

"Thank you for the food. I'm going to find Sherry. You have work to do, don't you?" As if summoned, Matt and Ramon appeared and slung their arms around him, nodding their heads. "Then get to it. No slacking off today." She left after that, not concerned with the pitiful whine that followed after her.

Chapter 12

Hello my lovely readers! Thank you to everyone who's made it this far. I'm so happy you guys like it so far! I had a free moment so I decided to go ahead and upload this week's chapter. So without further ado, on with the story!

It had been almost a year now since Ana began to live with the pack. She had been made the official Luna, although the bond hadn't been completed yet. They still searched to find a way around the problem, since no one wanted to let them complete the bond and risk their alpha's safety. The pack had been in an uproar at first. They'd grown to love and accept Ana. The fact that she was essentially a walking forbidden fruit was devastating. It wasn't until Taito reminded them they were a warrior pack, and there's nothing they hadn't defeated yet, that the pack was able to get back on their feet and come together to help find a solution.

However, the strain of not claiming his mate was taking its toll. Both Ana and Taito became progressively more irritable. They also could no longer stay in the same room as each other for long. Taito's wolf took over for longer periods. It was manageable at first, but now it was all everyone could do to make it through another day. Ana could stay long enough to calm him down, but she'd have to leave soon after, throwing him into another frenzy. The pack was at its whit's end with the alpha couple.

"Hang on a bit longer Taito. We're close. I know it." Taito had been moved to the infirmary. The doctor had finally decided to sedate him. Ana had snuck in shortly after everyone but a few night shift workers had left. She assumed it was fine since he was unconscious. I'll leave in the morning. I needed to see him. The bond had grown restless, creating an ache in her bones that only went away in his presence. Ana sighed and stole a quick glance around the room. He's asleep. It's fine, right? She began to climb into the bed next to him, but her hand slipped halfway. Ana flopped ungracefully on top of him, her limbs spread everywhere. She coughed awkwardly before attempting to get up. I was better off in the chair. While Ana was cursing her clumsiness, Taito's eyes were slowly opening. He'd been unconscious until his wolf stirred, sensing their mate. ...Ana? What's she doing here? Couldn't resist me perhaps? His wolf mirrored his smirk. Seems so, but I'm taking it from here. You've had plenty of time with her, and I've waited long enough. Wait! Damien! Have you forgotten about the wolfsbane? Plus, we can't bite her! We haven't officially asked yet. Kidnapping doesn't count. We told her she was. And look, she came to us all on her own. We won't last much longer if we don't her claim her now. I'm doing this for all of us – wolfsbane be damned. Damien cut the connection, smirking wider when he realized the position they were in. Ana didn't even have time to gasp before Damien had flipped them over.

"W-what? But you were...asleep..." Ana's breath caught when their eyes locked. The liquid gold glowing in Taito's eyes took her breath away. He grinned down at her.

"Pleasure to finally meet you my dear. I'm Damien, Taito's wolf."

"Uh, hi there? Mind getting off me Damien?" He only smirked and pressed closer, stopping when his lips met her neck.

"Sorry about this love, but I've waited long enough."

"What –" Ana was cut off by Damien sinking his teeth into her neck. She screamed and cried, the pain filled tears blurring her vision. He pulled back and licked the wound, effectively closing it. The pain faded, but tears continued to leak from her eyes. Damien reached to wipe them but she slapped his hand away. "Why did you do that?! You just put yourself in danger!"

"Ana I'm fine –"

"You're not! And no one said anything about you biting me until I bled! I should've known though when everyone complained about me blood, huh? That's sick. Don't touch me. I need time. That pain was ridiculous. And I know you're not, but it felt like I was being attacked by a monster. I need time to sort all of this out." Damien whimpered but nodded, pulling back and laying back on the bed. He turned his back to her as she walked out, softly closing the door. He wished she would have slammed it.

Chapter 13

Ana avoided him like the plague. Her bite mark had healed two days ago, but she refused to see him, let alone speak to him. Even in all her anger, she couldn't help but admire the mark. It had become an intricate tattoo – a midnight black wolf curled protectively around a golden key. When it had been discovered, the pack celebrated. Their alpha was alive and well – sulking didn't count – and their Luna had accepted him as her mate. The fact that the tattoo appeared was proof of that. They had completed the bond, unconventionally, but their relationship was suffering and strained at best. Ana practically flew from the room whenever Taito was near. They could sense when the other was close, and both were using it to their advantage. Because their goals were complete opposites, however, it was little more than a tiring game of cat and mouse.

"Why don't you stop running and jump him already?" Sherry managed to corner Ana one morning after breakfast. Uncaring of her protests, she'd dragged her off, shoving her in her room before following and locking the door. The lock had just been turned when the girls simultaneously turned to glare at each other, arms crossed.

"Let me out this instant."

"No. You're not leaving until you admit you love him." Ana's glare intensified before she sighed and sat on the bed.

"Honestly, it's not like I don't."

"Then what's the problem?"

"He didn't ask me! He bound me to him forever and didn't even care whether I was ready or not. I would've said yes. But this whole time I've felt powerless – like my desires and feelings didn't matter. And you know what? They obviously don't." Ana's eyes hardened and she stood, brushing off imaginary dust. Sherry waved her hands, trying to get the conversation back in the direction she was hoping for.

"Ana, wait. You have to understand –" Ana snapped her head up so quickly Sherry was afraid she'd gotten whiplash.

Understand? That what? Taito's wolf Damien forced us into this? That none of you can resist your urgeslong enough to ask a simple yes or no question? 'Oh I'm sorry, my wolf made medo it.'" Ana let out a bitter laugh before squeezing past her, unlocking thedoor, and stepping through. She stopped just long enough to speak one finaltime. "You know, eventually, that excuse is going to get old." She walkeddownstairs and out the door, not looking back once. Sherry sighed and left theroom, heading for Taito's office. How didit go so wrong?

Hello everyone! I know it's short but trust me, things are going to be heating up soon! I'm excited to see where this story takes us, since it's already getting a life of its own. This is my first published story that I've stuck with, so any and all feedback is welcome! See ya next chapter - bluesapphire out

Chapter 14

Hello lovelies! Sorry about the slow update, this week was kinda hectic for me. But I did say I'd try to update once a week and technically this week isn't over yet! So here it is, the highly anticipated next chapter!

"You'll need to take her some place nice. She needs to know you did all this because she's Ana and that her opinions matter. This is why we have the beta and gamma roles. You'll spend the entire day getting to know each other and then bam! You'll ask her to marry you and then you'll have children and then I'll be a god mother and - "

"Sherry! Let's just focus on the first part okay?" Taito, Matt, Ramon, Sherry, and Mary were currently plotting in Taito's office. Ana had regressed to the polite way of handling everyone that she'd used the first few months of being there. She was especially distant with the alpha - who had been sulking ever since. Sherry had saved the day by explaining why she was acting that way. She never said he couldn't have help. They had been scheming through the night, trying to make the plan perfect.

"Don't be yourself and everything should be fine." Ramon and Sherry snickered at that - whistling innocently when Taito turned to glare at them.

Matt gave him a reassuring pat on the back before shoving him out the door.

Taito had spent the last ten minutes trying to convince Ana to open the door so they could talk. She'd refused - whatever he had to say he could say it through the door. He crossed his arms, annoyed, and debated whether or not he should break it down instead. But then I'd have to get it fixed. Man this is such a drag. I just had to get such a stubborn woman as my mate. He counted to five before twisting the doorknob so hard he broke the lock. Ana stood on the other side, dumbfounded.

"Did you just...?" He shrugged and made himself comfortable on the bed, folding his hands behind his head.

"You wouldn't let me in. I need to ask you something important." She opened her mouth to speak, but closed it at his serious gaze. She had never seen him that serious, and all at once she was reminded of the alpha warrior he was. Has he always been that hot? Wait, wait! Focus before you miss the question. Stupid hormones.

"A-and? What is it?" Way to play it cool, Ana. Taito sat up and cleared his throat. He trapped her in his gaze, and Ana desperately tried to look away. The love shining in his eyes was too much to take in all at once.

"Will you go on a date with me?" She blinked, looked around the room, and pointed blankly to herself.

"You mean me?"

"There's no one else here." He deadpanned. Ana grinned, excitedly grabbing his hands. She would never admit it, but she'd missed him. The only thing holding her back was her pride, and the fact that he didn't seem to care for her opinion. But a date? That was perfect.

"When?"

"Right now." Maybe not.

"Right now?! Don't you know you've got to give a girl advance notice for a date?! I have to do my hair! It's too late for my nails. The outfit too...where are we going?"

"It's a surprise." Ana pushed him out of the room, giving him a quick peck on the cheek before closing the door. Taito smirked, swaggering down the stairs and back into his office. As soon as the others saw how obviously pleased he was Sherry was off. Matt and Ramon nodded their congratulations before sharing a look. It was Ramon who took one for the team and addressed the problem. He coughed to get the alpha's attention before gesturing to his outfit.

"You're not wearing that are you?" Taito waved off their concern.

"Of course not." He walked to the walk-in closet in his office, pulling out a set of clothes before stripping. Ramon's eye twitched, but Matt spoke up.

"You already had an outfit prepared? What if she'd said no?" Taito looked over and smirked, rolling up his sleeves.

"Who could resist this?"

Author's Note:

And there you have it folks! Points to anyone who caught the Naruto reference I slipped in there. If you liked this, or any other, chapter hit that like button! And feel free to leave comments! But pm me any constructive criticism, I'd rather not have that just chillin in my chapters. I hoped you liked this short but sweet chapter. Will the alpha couple grow closer, or will Ana's pride get in the way? Find out next time on Dollhouse! bluesapphire out.

Chapter 15

Taito was ready to drag Ana downstairs and throw her in the car. He never realized just how long it took women to get ready. He stood, preparing to take her now no matter what she was wearing when she and Sherry walked down the stairs. His breath caught. She was dressed in an off the shoulder black crop top with the word punk stretched enticingly over her chest. She'd paired it with distressed jeans and tan ballet flats. Gold bangles matched the gold lettering on her shirt and the medium sized hoops in her ears. Her makeup was light – deep red lipstick that accentuated her full lips and eyeliner to bring attention to her naturally sultry orbs. Her natural curls had been left alone. He realized he'd been staring when she began to rub her arm – a sign of nerves.

"If I look weird, I can go change – "

"No way!" Sherry and Taito shouted at the same time. Taito grabbed her hand and walked out, growling at the cat calls from his pack.

"You look amazing. Now get in the car we have places to be and I'd rather not be old and grey by the time we get there." Ana grinned and slid in the car, noting how he opened her door for her. Not bad, but knowing him I should wait before getting any more excited.

"Oh wow." Taito had taken her to a park. She'd been skeptical at first – she wasn't much of an outdoors kind of girl. He'd lead her down a worn path that emptied out into a beautiful clearing. There was a hill at the edge of the clearing, overlooking a distant town. The trees were an array of oranges, reds, and yellows. They'd stopped along the way to get picnic supplies, and by the time they'd gotten there the sun was setting.

While Ana had been admiring the view, Taito had set up the picnic, discretely patting his pockets once he'd finished. Ana sat down after she was done taking in the scenery, gasping again at the way he'd arranged everything. It was mostly simple food; the fanciest thing they had was sparkling cider (Taito had wanted wine but Ana didn't drink). Somehow, everything had been arranged like a buffet, with the appetizers first. Ana grinned again, fully relaxing for the first time since she'd been taken. They talked and laughed while they ate, getting to know the basic things about each other. This is what we should've done to begin with. I probably would've warmed up to him faster. Oh well. Better late than never. Once they finished they cleaned up, opting to stay a bit longer. Taito cleared his throat, gaining Ana's attention. He took a deep breath before beginning.

"We're not a normal couple, and I realize I did a few things out of order and without your consent. I apologize, but I don't regret my actions. However, I want you to remain by my side by your own choice, for the rest of our lives, and so I want to ask you something." He reached into his pocket and gestured for her to stand. Ana was so stunned she did so without complaint. He pulled out a long box and opened it, revealing a breathtaking sapphire pendant on a simple gold chain. He stood up and moved to stand behind her, the pendent in his hands. "This has been passed down through my family for generations. It's given to the Luna, or alpha female, and is a sign of true acceptance of the bond. Will you accept this, Ana?" He stayed still behind her, letting his words sink in. Tears gathered in her eyes as she processed all he had explained to her.

"Will you put it on for me?" The pure joy on his face when he did, turned her around and spun her cemented in her mind that she'd made the right decision. He set her down and cupped her face, leaving forward until their foreheads touched.

"One day I'll give you a matching ring. You'll be mine in every sense of the word." Her watery laugh was her only reply.

Chapter 16

Hello my lovely readers! Life has been hectic, but I'm back with another chapter! Thank you so much to everyone who's given this story a try. Now without further ado, on with the story!

Her last piece of resistance had crumbled after their date, and now they truly acted like mates. Ana still wasn't fully comfortable with all the physical contact, but she was gradually warming up to it. Taito had also figured out how much he affected her, especially when he deepened his voice. She'd turn to putty in his hands, and he teased her relentlessly for it. Ana had also apologized to the pack for her distant behavior. They'd brushed it off though; no one could stay angry when she apologized so sincerely. The pack had also gotten stronger. Taito had received a strength boost when Ana had accepted him as her mate. Because their alpha grew stronger, the pack did as well. Training became more intense. Ana joined the pack, and after bribing Taito, threw herself into the midst of their training sessions. She was surprisingly fierce, using her enhanced senses, speed, assumptions made by her opponent, and quick thinking to her advantage. It also helped that she'd taken self-defense classes before her abduction, so her body still remembered some of the moves. The proud gleam in Taito's eyes also pushed her to continue to come back to training. No one ridiculed her outright either. In fact, she earned their respect through her serious sparring and determination. They had stopped taking it easy on the first day when she proved her worth. They didn't train her as hard as a wolf, but they definitely pushed her limits.

It was after one such training session that Ana found herself exhausted but proud in the game room with Sherry. She'd managed to almost take down her sparring partner, Serenity, until she had regained her balance at the last moment. Still, her improvements were obvious, and that alone was enough to bolster her confidence. Sherry suddenly stood, her face twisting in alarm.

"What's wrong?" Sherry quickly grabbed her arm and pulled her into a closet, burying her under various jackets. Ana sputtered and flailed.

"Sherry what the frickety frack, knick knack – "

"I'll be back in a bit okay? Don't come out of the closet Ana. Do you hear me? And don't make a sound." The quiet click of the closet door and her fading footsteps let Ana know she was alone – for the moment anyway. She hunkered down and waited, counting sheep and making up stories about the coats currently smothering her to death. Wait a minute! I should be out there with my pack! I'm their Luna! She listened hard and counted slowly to ten before quietly busting out of the closet. Alright, let's do some surveillance. She tiptoed through the hall to the nearest room, the mission impossible theme song playing in her head. Holy ham and cheese! The sight that greeted her was gruesome. Wolves lay strewn about the part of the backyard she could see. Her pack fought over and around the dead bodies, unfazed by the carnage. She'd never seen all of them in wolf form, so she could only hope most of the bodies were the attackers. Well I can't directly in this fight. I'm no match for wolf. Maybe Sherry had the right ide – oh heck no! Screw fair fights Ana was looking for weapons. One of the younger members was fending off three wolves while protecting one of its injured comrades. Ana practically tore the room apart looking for some before moving to the next. Come on! There's gotta be something here. She rifled through the rest of the drawers before moving on to the closet. She moved everything, leaving nothing untouched. While moving the shoes, she caught sight of something shiny. Bingo! She shoved the shoes aside and pulled on the false bottom, revealing guns of all shapes and sizes, a few knives, and two pairs of nun chucks. What is this guy – an assassin?! But the nun chucks give off a more ninja feel. Focus Ana! Now is not the time. She dragged the gun case out first before hurriedly covering her discovery. Don't need unwanted guests finding this. She moved back to the window and surveyed the area again. The intruders were being pushed back, but some people were still being cornered. Ana turned back and looked through the collection, ignoring the small handhelds and going straight for the larger ones. She decided on an arm length one with a scope and what she assumed was a silencer. Ana set it up on the collapsible tripod stored next to it and took off the safety. All those spy novels and movies finally came in handy. She cracked the window just enough to clear her shots before settling in. she took a few deep breaths and aimed, thanking her lucky stars for the scope. Okay, you can do this. It's just like those arcade games. Just aim and fire. Be ready for the kickback. Although the arcade guns just shook and the deer weren't moving this much on the medium levels... She waited until one of the wolves crouched before firing. The kickback didn't knock her off her feet but it definitely bruised her shoulder. She scrambled to adjust the scope so she could see if she'd actually hit anything. The wolf had backed off and the battle had paused. Everyone was trying to figure out where the shot had come from. Ana was using the scope to see everything, and when she swept to the outskirts of the battle near the tree line she saw him. He was crouched low, watching the battle. She swore he looked right at her because as soon as she spotted him he winked and faded into the trees. Ana did a few more sweeps, but the man was nowhere to be found. The other wolves began to retreat as well. Ana figured mystery man was their leader, since they'd begun to leave shortly after he did. She sighed and sank down, about to drop the gun when a floorboard creaked. Ana abandoned the makeshift sniper and grabbed two handheld guns instead. She kicked everything else under the bed and moved behind the door. She held her breath as heavy footsteps approached. They stopped in front of the door, pushing it open slowly. Ana knew her scent had been all over the room now, so they couldn't use that to find her just yet. The intruder walked into the room, and as soon as he made it to the middle of the room she stepped from behind the door, guns raised.

"How did you get in here?" The man slowly turned around, a teasing smirk dancing across his lips.

"Through the front door of course." Ana froze, not wanting to believe what her eyes were telling her.

"You. But you're – "A harsh blow to the back of her head cut off her sentence. The man grinned wider and bent down, softly caressing her face.

"Oh, my dear, like I would ever let you go." He stood back up and walked out, Ana being carried by the one who'd knocked her out. They walked through the front door and into the forest, the guards already taken care of.

EX

Chapter 17

Hello lovelies! I've decided to update now since this week is about to get hectic. That's some craziness our girl Ana has gotten into huh? I mean poor girl just can't catch a break. Things'll be heating up from this point on so strap yourselves in and enjoy!

Ana awoke in a daze. She snuggled back under the satin sheets, wanting to forget her nightmare. This is why I hate silk – it's so slippery. Feels great until you wanna use it to block the cold. Ana turned over, trying to adjust so she could go back to sleep. Something was nagging at the back of her mind – fuzzy enough she couldn't grasp it, but clear enough it wouldn't leave her alone. She huffed and gave up on sleep, going to the closet to pick out some comfy clothes. The closet consisted of ball gowns, different costumes one usually only saw on Halloween, and various sleepwear. What the what? Where am I?! She shut the closet doors and looked around. The room was all dark colors, with the only window obscured by heavy blood red drapes. The bed was a king-sized canopy painted midnight blue. A thick black, fluffy rug laid on the floor on the right side of the bed. A blood red vanity took up a corner of the room, between the exit and bathroom door. The closet was styled like a wardrobe, made from dark mahogany wood. Everything was polished and seemingly new, so nothing explained why she was here. Even the bathroom followed the dark theme. The counters were marble, while the sinks were stainless steel appliances. There was an open shower further in. it was modeled to mimic a small cave, with the shower head in the middle made to rain straight down. The entire bathroom floor was heated, and a marble tub sat in the middle of the room. It was sunken into the floor, with steps leading in on both sides of the tub. Ana was impressed. No reason I can't enjoy the shower before trying to make my escape.

An hour later, now refreshed and awake, she decided it was time to leave. She picked the Lara Croft costume after much debate, since that costume gave her the most mobility. Her black and red shorts ended in the middle of her thighs, with her combat boots starting just below her knees. The top was a simple red corset with black strings. It had detached sleeves which began slightly above her elbow and ended at her wrists. Black fingerless gloves completed the outfit. Ana looked herself over in the mirror, turning this way and that to try to see the full effect. It's a bit more revealing than how I normally dress but it'll do I guess. I could've sworn Lara wore a different outfit though. She left the room and turned right, glancing around. The place reminded her of a gothic castle, although it seemed rather small for a castle. The hallway was long but narrow, and she passed mostly windows while she walked. The right side had the stereotypical floor to ceiling windows, while the left was littered with paintings. The paintings were all depicting wolves – some were on the battlefield while others were standing or sitting. It was creepy because all of their eyes seemed to be following her, causing Ana to quicken her pace. She made a beeline for the door at the end of the hall, throwing the doors open when she got there. She stopped dead in the doorway, rage and fear making her numb. There he sat, lazily sprawled across a marble throne. Two other men stood on either side, positioned at the bottom of the stairs. Ana only had eyes for him however, so she paid no mind to the overall set up of the room. His eyes lit with happiness upon her arrival. He descended the stairs and made his way towards her. She knew it was futile but she lunged at him anyway – immediately getting taken down by the muscle. The man chuckled and cupped her face.

"You're even more beautiful than the rumors suggest. Just as feisty though." Ana looked at him, confused and angry.

"Don't act like you don't know me Calvin! Not after what you did!" Calvin's eyes flashed with pain before he gripped her harder, making her wince.

"My name is Ivan, Calvin's younger twin brother. I can see why you'd be confused. But I can assure you I'm the better looking of the two." He winked and walked over to the window, clasping his hands behind his back. "However, your mate killed my brother and that just won't do. I could you, but that would be so cliché don't you think? No, I've thought of a fun little game instead. But we can't play until your mate gets here I'm afraid. Have you completed the process?" When she stubbornly refused to answer, Ivan snapped his fingers. One of the men wrenched her head painfully to the side, exposing her neck and thus her bite mark. Ivan turned to look at them, smirking when he saw the man nod. "Excellent! I knew you wouldn't let me down. This will also speed up his finding you. I've got to prepare!" He turned away and walked off, disappearing behind his ridiculously gaudy throne. Ana huffed, but obediently followed the henchmen back to her room. She sighed as they closed the door behind her, the fight in her long gone. Well I guess I'm trapped. Again. Am I a magnet for stuff like this? Because this has happened way too much. She propped herself up on the bed and looked toward the tv, examining the various games and consoles. She stopped when she spotted a few dance games. She popped one in and slid the Wii remote strap on her wrists as the first song began. Might as well have some fun while I wait.

Chapter 18

Ana grew bored after three days of being there. Ivan would visit her sometimes, bringing food and attempting to tell her his "tragic backstory." Ana tuned him out after his first visit – he droned on anyway. Today was her fourth day of captivity. She'd gone with the Little Red Riding Hood costume today. It was one of the less revealing options, and she had a feeling Taito was close. Ivan must have sensed it too, because he summoned her to the throne room around noon. He had his goons force her to her knees as soon as she stepped into the room. She glared daggers at him, making him chuckle. He tilted her chin up, inching closer.

"Such a shame we had to meet under these circumstances my dear." He forced a kiss on her and punched her in the gut so her mouth opened in a gasp. He took advantage, and Ana felt herself swallow. He pulled back and the henchmen released her. She grabbed her throat and stared at him accusingly.

"What did you do?!" He smirked and walked back to his throne, stretching lazily before sitting down, looking much too pleased with himself. Everyone in the room held their breaths, waiting to see what would happen next. Ana locked eyes with Ivan, about to open her mouth to demand an answer, when she noticed the changes in her body. It started in her toes first, slowly spreading up from there. The numbness crept up her body, holding it like a vice. Eyes wide, she could only continue to stare as her body slumped to the side. Her brain was next, wiping clean like a whiteboard at the end of a school day. Her eyes dulled, showing the transformation was complete. After a few moments she blinked, confused, and looked around struggling to gain control of her limbs. Ana took a few deep breaths, slowly pushing herself into a sitting position before addressing the other occupants in the room.

"Where am I? Who are you?" Ivan meanwhile could barely contain his glee at the turn of events. He hadn't been sure if his serum would work, but judging by the last few minutes he had been largely successful. And just in time too. I almost didn't complete it in time. His amusement grew when he noticed her eyes kept shifting to the door. Looks like all her memories weren't erased. Good. It wouldn't be fun otherwise. That bite mark should help the game along too. Poor Ana; she'll be attracted to a man and have no idea why. Her mind had forgotten, but her body knew when her mate was close. He cleared his throat and beckoned her forward.

"Now dear, don't tell me you forgot about me. We're about to be married after all." He had her sit in the throne next to his, kissing her hand and holding up a breathtaking diamond and sapphire ring. "You even left your ring in our room. You've got to stop being so distracted, love." Ana examined the ring once he slipped it on, turning it this way and that.

"Sorry, I must really be out of it if I can't remember any of this." Her gaze again slid to the door, but she wasn't sure what she was hoping for. There was a fog that clouded her mind. She felt like she was forgetting something important, but what that was she didn't know. "Why don't I remember you if we've known each other long enough to get married?" She looked at him skeptically, and he nodded, lacing their fingers.

"You were in a terrible accident a few days ago. There were no serious injuries other than a concussion. The doctors warned me of the possibility of amnesia. You should regain your memories in due time." The lie was smooth as it fell from his lips. She nodded, seemingly appeased by that answer. He stood and pulled her with him, releasing her to caress her face. He leaned down, tilting her chin up. Ana stood passively, believing it was fine even as disgust flooded her system. The distance continued to close between, and just as their lips were about to touch, the doors burst open. The last player had arrived.

So? What do you think? Poor Ana can't catch a break and now she's been essentially brainwashed! Just who is the last player? Are they alone? Until next time my wonderful readers! Have a great rest of the week and a safe weekend!

Chapter 19

I van clicked his tongue in disdain and pulled back, interlocking their fingers. He gazed down at his guests, amused. Taito was practically foaming at the mouth. He drew himself up to his full height, commanding attention.

"Return my mate to me at once, and your death will be swift." Ivan chuckled darkly as guards flooded the room. Taito and the warriors he'd brought got into defensive positions, his eyes never leaving Ivan's.

"I assure you, she's quite comfortable where she is." Ivan turned and yanked on their locked fingers, pulling her to him. He tilted her head up, giving her a long, passionate kiss. Ana stood perfectly still, neither resisting nor reciprocating. He must be telling the truth if he even had a ring. Who would go so far for a lie? But if that's the case...why does this feel so wrong? They broke apart, and Taito snapped. He roared so loud and viciously everyone cowered. Ana felt her body tingle, as if responding to it. She tilted her head, confused, and absentmindedly rubbed her neck, feeling what seemed to be a tattoo. Taito's eyes locked on the movement, slowly prowling forward. Ana watched him approach, entranced, until a hand on her arm yanked her back.

"Can't have you getting too friendly with my fiancé now." Taito growled when he spotted the rock on her finger; his entourage gasped.

"What have you done to her?" His expression was grim yet fierce. Those fathomless eyes trapped her like a deer in headlights. There was something achingly familiar about them – but again she didn't know what. The mark on her neck burned hotter the longer that man's eyes were on her. Ana narrowed her eyes. She opened her mouth to speak but Ivan beat her to it.

"I've simply reminded her of our life together. Amnesia can be a real kicker sometimes." He waited until the blood drained from his face. Until he slowly reached out to touch her. Only then did he press the button hidden in his coat pocket. The trap door below them activated, sending the warriors to the dungeons. Ana watched as it closed, not able to shake the look that man had given her. Who was that? "Ana." She turned toward Ivan, still slightly suspicious of him. "Come. The night is still young and we have much to do."

He lead her down a series of hallways with so many twists and turns she knew she'd get hopelessly lost if she ever came this way by herself. They finally stopped in front of a simple oak door, the lone guard nodding at them. He held the door for her and she nodded her thanks after stepping inside. The room was surprisingly simple given the rest of the place. A bland four poster bed sat on one side near a window, a simple oak bedside table and dresser near it. Two doors, one leading to a walk-in closet and the other leading to the bathroom, took up the wall on the other side. Inside the closet was an array of sleepwear and costumes similar to what she currently sported. Did I always go for men who were into this? I can see once or twice, but there are no regular clothes to speak of. The main event in the bathroom was the self-heated jacuzzi style tub sitting regally in the middle of the room. Steps lead into the tub, and two columns on either side protruded from the tub, with shower heads attached in twisting spirals that came together a few feet away from the columns so the water rained straight down. An assortment of bath bombs, soaps, hair products, and various sponges and luffas lined the cabinets. Stocked in the towel closet were fluffy pink, green, and blue towels in various shades. A small table sat near the tub, so one could put snacks or a laptop there while they relaxed. Well butter my biscuits. We must be a couple if he made sure the bathroom had everything I could possibly ask for. Heck, there's even a small spa like area for when I want to do my nails. She walked back out into the bedroom and draped her arms over his shoulders. She was behind him, so she missed the Cheshire grin rapidly spreading across his face.

"Have your memories begun to come back?" She pressed a chaste kiss on his temple before grabbing some pajamas and heading back into the bathroom.

"No, but you obviously know me so I believe you until something proves I shouldn't." The running water masked his victorious cackles.

o[!

Chapter 20

T aito growled, annoyed, as he looked around at his pack mates. They were all in different cells, and he was one of the few still awake. He paced his cell, trying and failing to reach out to Ana. Something was blocking his mental advances, adding to his ever – growing frustration. Things had finally started looking up – he should've known the universe would spite him.

"What happened to the Luna?" Everyone was quiet, trying to piece together the mystery. Suddenly, a teasing voice spoke up.

"I don't know, but did you see what she was wearing?" Loud, appreciative whistles were quickly silenced by the alpha's jealous roar. One of his warriors, Stephen, rubbed his neck sheepishly.

"We meant no harm alpha. Just trying to lighten the mood." Taito huffed, appeased, and went back to pacing.

"Use someone else's mate to do so then." Snickers rose from the cells. Eventually they tapered off, and silence washed over them once more. Taito collapsed on the rickety bed with a sigh, his heart clenching in pain. I'll save you. Just wait for me.

Ana awoke the next morning refreshed but empty. She couldn't forget that man's eyes. The emotions that'd swam there hit her hard. She was filled with longing, just at the thought of his haunting gaze. *My lover is right here, so why are my thoughts so consumed with the other? Maybe a past love I haven't seen in a long time?* She abandoned her train of thought once a massive headache began the longer she'd tried sorting it out. After getting ready for the day, she resolved to find and question the man herself. Ana knew they were here somewhere – Ivan had explained last night he'd sent them to the underground cells. *I just need to find those and get this mess straightened out. Easier said than done though.* Determined, Ana walked to the wardrobe and lazily browsed through outfits. These were skimpier than she initially thought. She finally decided on the costume labeled huntress. It was a skin tight black body suit that connected at the waist by a belt, so it could break into two separate pieces when needed. There was a diamond cut out in the front and back, with the larger diamond at the back. Rips in the pants started above her knees and continued down to her ankles. It was sleeveless, and she paired it with black ankle boots. It also came with a cloak, but she saw no reason to wear that. She walked around the room, getting used to the feel of the material. Once she was satisfied, she left the room, noting the guard was no longer there. She walked slowly, trying to remember how to get to the foyer. *Maybe it's one big circle, so if I keep going right I'll eventually end up somewhere I recognize.* The hallways seemed never ending, and by the time she stumbled upon the kitchen, Ana felt like she'd been wandering for hours. She almost cried when she saw the wide array of food that was sitting on the kitchen counter. The bread and pies especially smelled freshly baked, so the chef probably stepped out for a minute. She walked up to the cupboard, searching until she found the plates. She grabbed one and danced over to the pile of French toast, plucking two from the pile. She was hit with a fleeting sense of déjà vu, but it faded as soon as Ana sank her teeth into her prize. She almost moaned at the taste, devouring the treat until nothing remained. She went back for fruits and orange juice until she was full. She cleaned everything when she was done and set off again, her spirits high once more.

Ana again felt like she'd been walking for ages. She had long given up on her search for the cells and instead trying to find her way back to her room. She rested her hand on the wall beside her, but stumbled when her hand sank into it along with the panel. She stared, dazed, as a hidden stairway slowly revealed itself. She stood at the top, squinting into the darkness to try to see where it lead. She had taken a step towards it when she stopped herself, caught in an internal debate. Some shady stairway literally pops up out of nowhere and you want to go down there? This has typical scary movie victim scene written all over it. But I am curious...and it may be the entrance to the underground cells. But curiosity killed the cat. And what if the entrance closes... That thought made her step back. She was just about to turn around before hands shot out and dragged her back, shoving her into the staircase. Ana turned and pounded on the now closed wall, near hysterical.

"What's the big idea? Open this back up! Let me out of here!" On the other side, the perpetrator glanced behind him, rolling his eyes at Ivan.

"Won't this speed up her recovery?" Ivan shook his head at the man's lack of imagination.

"There's no fun in this if I don't dangle her in front of him, only to snatch her back at the last minute. Who knows – I may even keep her for myself after this." Whistling, Ivan walked away. The man stayed a bit longer, glancing back at the hidden stairwell. Poor girl. She sure has bad luck to get mixed up with Ivan.

Hello my lovely readers! As always thank you for reading.

Chapter 21

Ana sighed and moved forward, placing one hand on the wall for balance. She moved slowly – the darkness made sure of that. "Would it kill them to put lights in here?" As soon as the word 'light' left her lips torches sprang to life. Ana blinked, stunned, before continuing. "I'm finding another exit and getting out of here. The medieval theme was cute at first but now this's all just weird." She huffed, annoyed, and turned left when she reached the bottom of the stairs. Now that lights had appeared, she took a look at her surroundings. The walls were a depressing slate grey concrete. Cobwebs decorated the ceiling corners. Torches continued to provide both heat and light, though how they did that when there wasn't a fire burning she didn't know.

Meanwhile, Taito was going crazy, believing he was hallucinating. He had picked up Ana's scent a few minutes ago, and it seemed to be getting closer. But there was no way she'd wandered down here by mistake, unless... His thoughts were interrupted when she rounded the corner, appearing at the end of the hallway. Her scent assaulted his senses, and alerted the rest of the warriors to her presence. Despite popular belief, all werewolf noses were not created equal. A werewolf's nose became especially powerful when their mate was involved. Alphas had the best sense of smell, then betas and trackers, and it decreased from there. Their noses were still much stronger than humans' however.

Ana took a deep breath, steeling herself, before marching determinedly through the hall, peering into the various cells. Every man she looked at nodded in respect, leaving her more confused. She found him at almost the end of the lineup. He stood, staring at her with wild, disbelieving eyes. A shiver ran through her at his intense gaze, but she refused to turn to jello just yet. She wanted answers, and she would get them. She just hoped she'd get them before her brain short circuited. Why did he keep looking at her like that? She crossed her arms and straightened her posture, eyes bright in a mixture of curiosity and defiance.

"Who are you to me?" The deafening silence did nothing for her confidence as he continued to stare. He swallowed hard, eyes darkening before he answered her.

"Your mate." She blinked, opening her mouth only to close it as she struggled to process what he'd said. Is this jerk making fun of me? This isn't some fairy tale! Ana rolled her eyes and tried a different approach.

"Where do I know you from? How did we meet?" He ignored the first question but answered the second, pride evident in his tone.

"I saved you from the dangerous man who was using you for his sick, twisted experiments." His anger had replaced the pride when he told her about the experiments. Ana's confusion grew at this revelation. That's not how she remembered it.

"No, I saved myself. Calvin had left the cell door open by mistake one night and I was able to escape. All those 'games' of hide and seek came in handy." Bitterness caused her to glare at the floor. Otherwise she would've noticed the surprise, confusion, and angered understanding flashing across Taito's face. So that's your game, is it? When I get my hands on him we'll destroy him. Ana was looking up again, tapping her thumb on her thigh. Taito knew that meant she was trying to make sense of something. Of course she would – her memories had been tampered with. She frowned harder, glancing between him and the way she'd come. "Maybe this was a bad idea after all. Even if you're telling the truth or lying it's not like I would know. I don't remember much and Ivan said that was because of my accident."

"Ana, you've never been in an accident." She glared, falling back on her default response – denial.

"And how would you know? I don't even know who you are which means that we either met recently and I forgot thanks to my amnesia or we met so long ago it's no longer relevant. You only popped up today so how would you know if I have or have not? This was a stupid idea. I shouldn't have come. I just wanted to know why every time you look at me it feels like I was shocked." She turned to go but his hand shot out, grabbing her wrist.

"Do you feel that?" Her surprised nod was all the answer he needed. "I'm a werewolf, and that tingle you feel is a sign that we're mates, destined for each other." Ana stared, transfixed, before reaching out her other hand to experimentally cup his face. Taito leaned into her hand, barely managing to bury the purr threatening to burst from his throat. The moment ended too soon when she pulled back, holding up her hand.

"If we're meant for each other, why did I accept this?" Taito looked stricken, but the moment passed so quickly she might have imagined it.

"That isn't real. I don't know where he got that from, but you belong to me." Heat coiled in her stomach at that last statement, but she ignored it to address the first.

"So what, he bought a fake ring and pretended to be my fiancé? What for?"

"To get to me." The bland look he received had him desperately backpedaling, but the damage was done.

"So, you're saying this is all some scam to get to you?" She stepped out of his grasp, shooting him a wounded look. "Am I so undesirable the only reason anyone would consider proposing to me would be to get to you?" She was backing away now, Taito desperately reaching for her through the bars.

"No! But we're mates. Everyone knows you're my weakness –"

"Your weakness?" Running an agitated hand through his hair he tried one last time.

"Ana –"

"No. I've heard enough." Turning on her heel she stomped back the way she'd come. When they could no longer hear her, Stephen spoke up.

"Maybe word it a bit better next time." Taito shot him a nasty glare before turning to sulk in his cell.

Hello my lovely readers! I apologize for the delay, and I know this probably isn't the update you were hoping for, but I needed to fix this slight error on my part before the story progressed any further. Chapter 23 was my last pre-written chapter, so I'm at a bit of a roadblock on where I want them to go from here. But fear not! The new chapter shall soon be out! Until next time!

Chapter 22

A na was furious. She had half a mind to go back down there and yell at the man until she was satisfied, but the weird tingling that happened just when he looked at her held her back. She hadn't told Ivan about what went on down in the cells, or even finding them. She'd even tried actually acting like a couple, but she couldn't bring herself to feel anything for him besides tolerance and mild annoyance. Had she really agreed to marry this man? But an entire scheme that revolved around a sham marriage proposal? She scoffed at the idea. No one's that crazy. That man is just messing with my head. Besides, just because I don't love Ivan doesn't mean he can't make me happy. He had to an extent. She was content so she couldn't really complain.

"Ana? Did you hear me?" She was snapped back to reality with the question.

"No, sorry. What did you say?" He smiled and tugged her forward so she was snuggled against him.

"You like it here don't you?" She sighed and shot him a small smile, not sure where he was going with this.

"Yes?"

"And I make you happy?"

"Yes..." There was more hesitance now. And were his canines always so sharp? He moved closer and tightened his grip, preventing her from moving.

"Then you shall be mine in every sense of the word." He closed the distance between them and kissed her, trailing down to her neck. She pushed him away when he kissed her tattoo, practically flying to the other side of the room.

"What are you doing?" He had never been this forward before, saying he would wait until she was more comfortable with him again. His advances now were setting off red flags. Adrenaline was being pumped into her veins and her body tensed, ready to spring at a moments notice. She waited until he began to inch closer once more before making a break for the door. His hand caught the bottom of her nightgown, tearing it in the process. Ana sped down the halls, not daring to look back. Ivan walked slowly to the bedroom door, the ripped fabric clutched firmly in his hands. He brought it to his nose and inhaled deeply, predatory eyes narrowing to slits.

"I always did love a good chase."

So what did you think? As always, thank you so much for taking the time to read my story and feel free to leave a comment! Until next time!

Chapter 23

T aito slammed his hands into the bars, hissing in pain shortly after. They had been laced with a thin coat of silver, so he was only affected when directly touching them. Apprehension had settled in his stomach and refused to leave. He'd felt slight pain trickle through the bond, meaning Ivan had touched his mark. After that her panic and wariness had flooded his senses, before the bond went alarmingly silent. He had been antsy ever since, causing his warriors to also be on edge. Pack wolves were finely tuned to their alpha's and luna's wolves. This is why the alpha and luna were so important. The alpha kept both the mental and physical strength of the pack grounded, which is why alphas couldn't rule successfully without a luna. If the alpha didn't have his luna to ground him, he'd slowly fall apart, taking the pack along with him. This also explained why if the acting luna died, the alpha would hand his role to his son, regardless of whether he was of the proper age. The retired alpha would help grow the new alpha into his role until he found his mate. Only then would the previous alpha fully retire and place the full burden on the new alpha. Because Ana was human, the warriors could only take their cues from Taito. Based on how agitated he was, they all knew something was wrong with the luna.

"What happened?" Taito was only half paying attention to his men, still trying to find his mate.

"I'm not sure. All I know is Ivan tried something that caused Ana to panic. I know she's still alive, but the bond is silent." Grim silence met his statement. The warriors shifted restlessly, every instinct telling them to help their luna, but with silver coated bars, that was easier said than done.

Ana ducked behind a bookshelf after stumbling upon the library. She barely breathed as she listened for Ivan's footsteps. They'd gotten lighter than his usual heavier gate. She worried her lip, cursing herself for picking an unfamiliar room to hide in, although technically every room besides their bedroom was unfamiliar to her. She'd initially chosen this room because of the cobwebs, and other signs of obvious disuse. However, she was running blind. She had no idea if Ivan was human or supernatural. Her tracks were easy enough to cover if he were human, but if he wasn't, Ana was at a huge disadvantage. She hadn't initially been this afraid, but apprehension had flooded her system, seemingly from an outside source. This had only escalated her own emotions, until her heart was pounding in her chest, keeping her adrenaline rush going. Her current plan was to make it back to the cells and have that jerk help her out. The other people worked for Ivan, so he and his friends were her only option. A creak in the floorboards had her instantly on alert. She had no idea if Ivan had employed the help of his men in his hunt for her, but she was certain they'd turn her in regardless if they found her. Ana had no idea what was in store for her if she was caught, but something told her it was nothing good. She waited with baited breath as the footsteps came closer. The person shuffled dangerously close to her hide away, and Ana wanted to scream at the anticipation as they continued searching. Go away, go away, please go away. Someone up there must have been listening, because the footsteps retreated shortly after her plea. She waited until the door closed to breathe a sigh of relief. She crept to the other side, searching blindly for an exit.

She moved painstakingly slow, trying not to bump into anything along the way. There was a door in the back corner, slightly hidden by one of the shelves. She opened it slowly, poking her head through the opening when it was wide enough. The coast was clear at the moment, so she didn't waste any time venturing into the hallway. She kept her hand pressed to the wall in hopes of activating the passageway. Ana kept wary eyes trained in front and behind her, not wanting to be taken by surprise. She was so focused on watching out for people however, that she missed the foreign object on the floor, causing her feet to fly out in front of her. Ana flailed, letting out an undignified squawk as she scrambled to find purchase on the walls. Her hand landed on the panel for the passageway, but couldn't prevent her fall. With a bruised tailbone, she stood and grinned in triumph, dusting herself off. Quickly, she wen down the stairs and rounding the corner, every instinct tuned to reach him. She barely registered the relieved looks on their faces as she set about opening the cell doors.

Chapter 24

<hr>

Taito couldn't help the flood of relief as soon as he caught her scent. His warriors practically barreled out of the cells as she unlocked and opened them. They congregated behind her, eyes flicking back and forth and muscles tense in preparation of a fight. As soon as she opened his cell he scooped her up into his arms, burying his nose in her hair to calm his frazzled nerves. Ana froze, but relaxed soon after, melting into the contact. This so isn't the time! Ana squirmed until he let her go, smoothing her outfit back down. Taito's eyes roamed her form until he was satisfied she wasn't severely injured. His eyes held so many emotions she looked away, opting instead to address the whole group. Inhaling deeply, she filled them in on her current situation, causing Taito to roar with anger. Her body practically sang in response, but she pushed that aside to deal with later. Taito balled his fists and chuckled humorlessly. "He wants to play? Then let's play."

Hey guys! Sorry for the wait and as always thank you so much for reading. See ya next chapter!

Chapter 25

Their confidence and bravado steadily wore down as time wore on. With no sign of Ivan and his goons, the wolves were getting increasingly agitated. Ana had led the group back to the library, where she'd last seen someone. However, the only sign of life was the disturbed dust. Confused, Taito had made the executive decision to prioritize Ana's safe return. That too, was proving difficult for the group.

"I'm pretty sure we're walking in circles. I thought you guys were supposed to be good at this stuff?"

"We are."

"Then why has no one been able to find the exit yet? There aren't any scents you can track back to the entrance? How did you guys even get in here?" Taito rolled his eyes and threw a glance over his shoulder at Ana before answering.

"Would you like to try?" Ana huffed and crossed her arms. He had her there.

"I found something!" One of the warriors shouted from the bend in the hallway. Everyone rushed over, but Taito positioned himself in front of

Ana just in case. Devin, the warrior who'd made the discovery, stood in front of an old, worn oak door. There was slight water damage lining the bottom. The door itself was decorated by a lone brass knocker. Ana shivered and shifted closer to Taito, only just feeling the slight breeze coming from the crack underneath the door. Devin pushed it open, but before anyone could step through Ana grabbed Taito's arm.

"Wait. Don't you think it's been a bit too quiet this whole time?" At the others' blank looks, she elaborated. "I mean, we weren't able to find anyone since I freed you from the cells. We couldn't find the exit either, and now all of a sudden there's a door that's clearly leading outside? None of you find this even a tad bit suspicious?" The others paused to consider her argument, before adopting grim looks.

"You're right. All of this could very well be a trap. But it's also a fact that we haven't found an exit besides this one, and we can't afford to waste energy turning around and potentially getting lost in this maze before we find another. This is our best shot." Everyone nodded in agreement before stepping through the open door. The sight that greeted them was not one they were expecting. Ana nearly screamed in frustration.

"Oh, you've got to be kidding me!"

Hello my lovely readers! School picked up, but I managed to find a small window to write and feed your curiosity after that short chapter. Enjoy your weekend!

Chapter 26

The sight that greeted them was anything but relieving. Water stretched for miles on three sides of what seemed to be an island that they found themselves on. The building took up most of the available space from what they could tell. The sun was already making its descent. It seemed to be around two or three in the afternoon, but a lack of boats wasn't what had them worried. It was the massive army standing between them and their only means of escape - a single road connecting the island and the rest of the world. Ivan stood at the forefront, smirking so wide it seemed his grin would split his face.

"The main attraction has finally arrived." Taito pushed Ana back the way they came, his eyes never leaving Ivan's.

"Go back inside. Barricade and lock the door if you can. I'll come get you when this is over."

"But-"

"Now is not the time. Do as I say so I can fight at full strength." Without another word she turned and reentered the building, closing the door firmly behind her. Taito relaxed slightly with his mate's safety assured, sliding into a fighting stance. He didn't have to tell his warriors to shift - they knew a fight when they saw one.

"Always one to cut right to the chase I see. It doesn't have to be this way you know. All I need is Ana, and your death will be swift." Taito's resounding roar was all the answer receivsed tot that demand. Ivan shook his head, utterly disappointed. "I'm sorry you feel that way. But if I can't have her...no one can." Vampires leaped into action, and Taito's warriors met them halfway. Teeth gnashed and bodies slammed into the ground as the battle commenced. Taito and Ivan stayed where they were, sizing the other up. "After I'm done with you, I'll go back in there and take my time. I'll torture her slowly, until she's begging me for death." Taito roared and threw himself at Ivan, who spun away at the last second, narrowly dodging claws. Laughter, shouts, and grunts were all one could here. The time for words was over. Limbs were torn, blood spurting like hellish rain as neither side gave in. Ivan and Taito focused solely on each other. Taito rushed him, getting in a swipe to the stomach before Ivan retaliated with a bite to the hind leg before rolling underneath.

Meanwhile, Ana paced, torturing herself with possible scenarios to explain the sounds on the other side of the door. Screams and the ripping of clothes were the most prominent, with the occasional growl or whimper thrown into the mix. What the heck is going on out there??

I just want to take a moment to thank everyone who has made it this far, and everyone who's given my story a chance. When I first posted this story, I never dreamed anyone would read it, much less all of you who have. Your reading this means the world to me! Thank you all so much! See ya next chapter!

Chapter 27

Maybe I should open the door a crack and see what's going on? But he said stay in here....But if I just peak out I'm technically still inside, right? Nodding her head and steeling her nerves, Ana pushed open the door a crack, before abruptly slamming it closed. A headless body had been heading straight for her. She let out a sob, sliding down the door and covering her ears. This is crazy! There's a whole supernatural fight and the only exit is being blocked by said fight! There's got a be another way out of here because there is no way I'm staying long enough to see how this all plays out. Standing on shaky legs, she began moving back the way they'd come, one hand permanently attached to the wall. Ana kept sharp eyes on her surroundings, trying to find another passage that could lead to the exit. She had been walking for what couldn't have been more than five minutes when she felt a chill race down her spine. She didn't even spare a glance over her shoulder to see what it was before sprinting down the hall. Her eyes raked over the walls, cursing her luck at the lack of any sort of defensive weapon. The chill increased, seconds before arms encircled her waist.

"Going somewhere my dear?" The man clicked his tongue before dragging her back towards the door leading outside. "The main event has only just begun. We can't have our star running out in the middle, now can we?"

Ana screamed and thrashed, but the man only chuckled, before throwing open the doors. The fighting was winding down at this point, with most of the vampires defeated. Taito and his warriors were panting as they finished the last of their opponents off, sweat and blood mingling on their bodies. None of them seemed to be too heavily damaged, however. But everyone paused to see the reason the doors had opened. Ana stood, still struggling, with her arms trapped at her side by the arm wound around her waist. One of the vampires had her neck pressed painfully to the side, fully exposing it. All he had to do was lean down slightly to make a meal of her - she was completely at his mercy. Taito growled a warning before stepping forward, only to be halted by Ivan.

"Now, now. We wouldn't want anything to happen to her because of any rash moves, now would we?" Taito's glare intensified, but the wolves stayed where they were. Ivan clapped his hands and moved back until he was right beside Ana, cupping her face. "Such flawless skin. It would be a shame if something happened to change that. Of course, that all depends on you." He turned back around and spread his arms wide. "Surrender to me and I'll let your woman go. If not, well I'll kill her slowly, draining every drop of blood in her body." Ana continued to squirm, but to no avail. She could tell her captor was starting to become irritated with all of her movements though. She wiggled until she could move her legs, then stomped hard on his foot. He flinched, and loosened his grip enough for her to shoot out of his arms. She made a mad dash for Taito, her arms reaching for him. He sprang at her, hands almost connecting until she was yanked back. Ivan tsked, his face changing to a maniacal grin. "I do hate when others interrupt. But since you want to die so bad..." He pushed her head to the side and bit down. Ana screamed and went limp, and all Taito saw was red.

"ANA!!!"

As always, thank you to my wonderful readers. Have a wonderful Thanksgiving and see you next time!

Chapter 28

I t felt like she was floating. She wasn't sure where she was, or how she got there. All she knew was it was dark and she felt weightless. Wait...where is everyone? What happened after Ivan bit me? A light appeared above where she was floating, but she was hesitant to go towards The feeling slowly returned to her limbs the longer she looked at it, shocking pain reverberating through her being. So maybe not that way... Ana... She turned in the direction of the voice, but that just had her in the direction of the light again. She shook her head, stubbornly turning her head away. No way disembodied voice. I don't wanna go that way. You can't stay here. This is no place for the living. The living? So this is the afterlife? It's....not as lively as it's made out to be. The voice chuckled before responding. This is only the gateway to the afterlife. What you picture lies on the other side. You. however, belong in the light my dear. Pain is temporary, or are you not as strong as I initially thought? If i had known you were such a quitter, well, I wouldn't have placed my hopes on you. Hey! I never said I was a quitter. She turned back towards the light, allowing it to grow steadily closer. Hey wait, what do you mean by ... She turned back but the voice was gone and the darkness grew colder as the light grew brighter. Nevermind. Light engulfed her senses and she closed her eyes.

"It's been almost two weeks since then, why hasn't she woken up yet?" Taito paced up and down the hallway, agitated by the lack of progress in Ana's treatment. He'd ripped Ivan's head from his body while one of the warriors caught Ana's crumbling form. It had been a race against time getting from there back to the pack house. The doctor has explained the mate bond and the fact that Ivan hadn't taken as much blood as they initially thought were what saved her life. It was most likely she passed out from the pain. The bruising and bite marks had started to fade by the first week, but she had yet to so much as twitch since being admitted to the hospital. The doctor advised for patience, especially considering her body was physically and mentally drained. Ivan had tampered with her memories, making the road to recovery that much slower as her body healed while her brain struggled to process the truths and lies it had been fed. Members of the pack came by, offering to watch their luna while Taito got rest but he refused, only taking the food after his beta finally broke through that he would be no good to Ana when she awoke if he was a disaster himself.

It was hitting the two week mark. Taito was looking over paperwork in the corner of the room where a desk had been set up when he felt it. A small tug at the back of his mind. His snapped over to the bed so fast he swore he got whiplash, but nothing compared tot he relief he felt when her hand twitched. He dropped the papers and practically flew to the side of the bed, grabbing her hand and giving it a comforting squeeze. He'd been talking to her throughout her stay with no changes or progress, so he held his breath as he waited for another sign of life. If she didn't pull through today, he wasn't sure how much longer he could successfully lead his pack. He squeezed again and waited, and this time, she squeezed back. It was weak, but it was there. His other hand came up to stroke her face. She moved into the gentle touch, her eyes moving behind her eyelids. Taito sat in the chair, lightly tickling her sides. She squirmed, weakly lifting her hand to bat away his prying fingers. As her eyes finally opened, irritation shining through her strong gaze despite her state, Taito collapsed on the bed. He didn't cry, he simply laid there, hunched over and holding her hand like his life depended on it.

"Still got that strong grip I see." Even her voice was weak, which wasn't surprising, but it was music to his ears. He felt his wolf emerge from the back of his mind, felt the weight lift from his shoulders. His Ana was back.

"Kept me waiting long enough." She grinned and winked before looking around the room for something to drink. He got the hint and poured her some water, helping her drink it when he got back to her side.

"Of course. What's a comeback if it's not dramatic?" His laugh rang through the hospital, alerting the staff who spread the news like wildfire as her doctor came sweeping into the room. Their luna was back.

Epilogue

Six years had passed since Ana's awakening. The pack had only grown stronger after the pair had finished the mating process. With their new status, the pack had become stronger than ever. Ana and Taito had two children. Alexandria was turning four while Jackson was turning one this year.

Word of Ivan's defeat had spread like wildfire. Packs and vampire covens alike were more wary of attacking the pack, bringing peace and harmony. Taito still had the warriors train and the pack patrolled, saying one could never be too careful. It was during one such peaceful night that the alpha family was curled up in their new house, the fireplace crackling softly in the background.

"The kids are asleep. The pack's taken care of, and we finally have everything we've ever wanted. I've got to admit - I never imagined things would turn out like this after you found me that night." Taito chuckled and ran his hands gently through her now short hair.

"I'm glad it did. You were definitely putting me through the wringer for a minute there. I wasn't sure if we'd get our happily ever after." Ana grinned up at him and placed a quick kiss on his lips, pulling away before he could deepen it. He opened his mouth to protest, but was cut off by a howl coming from the south perimeter. Taito groaned and Ana winked, both moving to fall into their roles in case of attack.

"Looks like that happily ever after will have to wait just a bit longer."